Original Korean text by Eun-gyu Choi
Illustrations by Ji-yeon Kim
Korean edition © Dawoolim

This English edition published by big & SMALL in 2015
by arrangement with Dawoolim
English text edited by Joy Cowley
English edition © big & SMALL 2015

Distributed in the United States and Canada by
Lerner Publishing Group, Inc.
241 First Avenue North
Minneapolis, MN 55401 U.S.A.
www.lernerbooks.com

ISBN: 978-1-925233-66-7

Printed in Korea

All Kinds of Nests!

Written by Eun-gyu Choi
Illustrated by Ji-yeon Kim
Edited by Joy Cowley

big & SMALL

The skylark builds a nest
by stacking dried grass
or sticks on the ground.

Hello, Skylark!
Your nest is cozy!

Yes, my little nest
is comfortable.

The skylark lays
about five eggs at a time.

She looks for food
walking with quick steps.

That's because the water gives me my food.

A kingfisher builds its nest by making a hole in a bank by the edge of the water.

Kingfisher, your nest is by the water.

The kingfisher looks
for food in the water.

When it sees its prey,
it swoops down to catch it.

The grebe builds its nest using reeds and water plants.

Hello, Grebe! I see that your nest is on the water.

Yes, it floats and protects my eggs.

Grebes have webbed feet.
They dive into the water
to feed on their prey.

A woodpecker makes its nest
in a hole in a tree.

Woodpeckers use their sharp beaks
to eat insects under the tree's bark.

They have sharp claws
that hang on to the tree.

15

Instead of making a nest,
the owl lives in a hollow tree
or a crack between rocks.

Owls fly at night to find prey.

An owl can turn its head around
to see directly behind it.

The magpie builds a nest in a tree by weaving sticks together.

Yes, and it has a round entrance.

Magpie, your nest is like a round ball.

Seen from above, the magpie's nest
looks like a solid round ball.
This is to protect the eggs
from hungry flying birds.

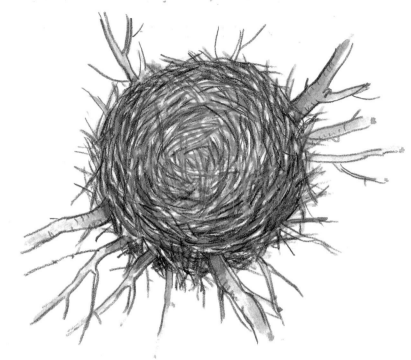

Magpies eat varied foods
including seeds, fruits,
insects, worms, scraps, and
small birds and eggs.

The male bowerbird
makes a nest on the ground.
He decorates it with fruit and flowers.

If the female bowerbird
likes the nest the male has made,
she will mate with him.

After mating, the female
will make another nest
for their young bowerbirds.

The swallow makes a nest
under the eaves of a building.
The nest is a mixture
of mud and straw.

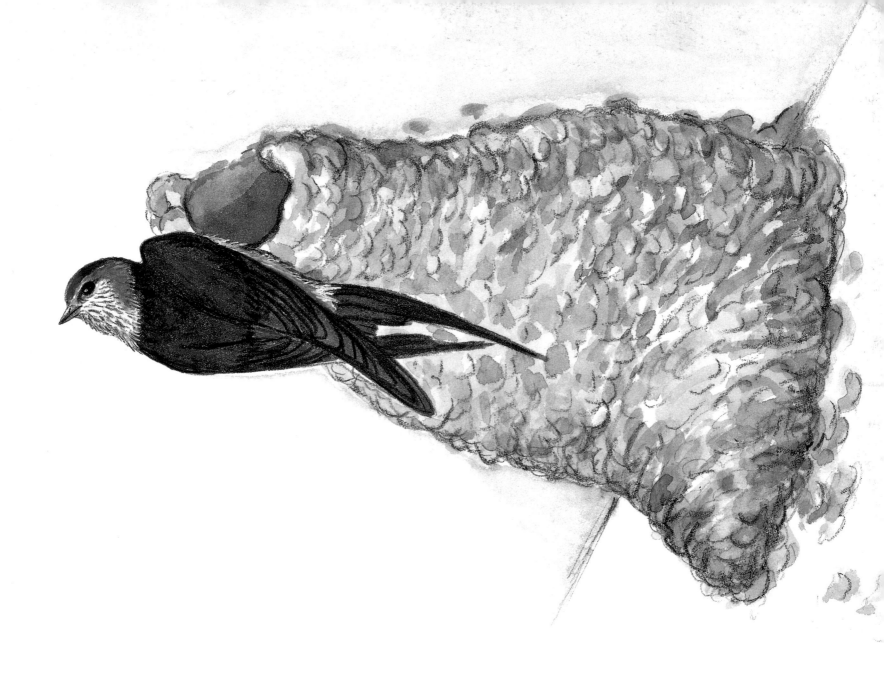

The nest has a very narrow entrance
to protect the babies from predators.

Which is the best nest?

Skylark's nest

Grebe's nest

Woodpecker's nest

Kingfisher's nest

All are best for the birds that made them.

Hummingbird's nest

Bowerbird's nest

Owl's nest

Swallow's nest

Ostrich's nest

Magpie's nest

All Kinds of Nests

Birds make nests that best suit their way of living. By studying their nests we can learn about their habits, nesting territories, materials used in nests and about eggs and mating habits.

Let's think

Why do birds build nests?

What are some of the things that influence the type of nest a bird builds?

What are some of the different types of nests that birds build?

How do birds protect their nests?

Let's Do!

Let's make a nest! Go on a nature walk to a park or nature reserve and observe any birds there you see. Find and collect materials in this habitat that you think birds would use to make their nests: dried grasses, twigs, leaves, scraps of paper, or other things.
Now, try to weave these materials together using a little mud (or glue) if necessary. Is it easy to make a bird nest?